This book belongs to

Leila

Written by Tim Bugbird.
Illustrated by Lara Ede.
Designed by Sarah Vince.

Katie the Candy Cane Fairy

Tim Bugbird · Lara Ede

make
believe
ideas

In a gingerbread house on Lantern Lane, decked in red, white, and green,

lived a singer, Katie Candy Cane –
Fairyland's Christmas queen!

Lantern Lane

With her fairy sisters, Crystal and Glo,
she worked throughout the year
to perfect their famous, festive show
and fill each song with cheer!

The secret behind the fairies' fame –
the music and sparkle and lights –
was extra-special candy canes
with magical red-and-white stripes!

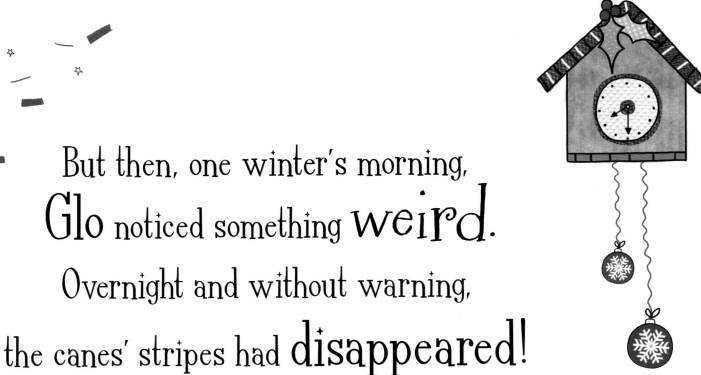

But then, one winter's morning,
Glo noticed something weird.
Overnight and without warning,
the canes' stripes had disappeared!

The shows were in their planner
and rehearsals were nearly through,
but with no stripes to create the glamour,
what would the fairies do?

Crystal said, "If we use our brains,
how difficult can it be
to put on a show **without** striped canes?
Let's give it a *try* and see!"

But with no flashes and fizzes,
or musical, magical stuff,
and a lack of sparkles and whizzes,
it just didn't feel good enough!

So the fairies jumped on their
motortrike
and raced to
Holly's cane store.

"I'm **totally out** of stripes,"
Holly said,
"and I know **I can't**
get any more!"

"I've got canes in gold with sparkly stars or silver with hearts and dots.

I've got a few in blue, and purple, too. Look around - I've got lots!

But just one thing I have not got – and that's without a doubt – is any kind of cane with stripes. I am totally, completely sold out!"

SOLD OUT

canes

Katie's poor head was in a spin,
her brain was in a tangle.
The fairies had to think again
to see things from a different angle.

So they searched their house
for their stripiest things –
for hats and scarves and socks.

They wore them together
with **stripes** on their **wings**
and their stripiest
party frocks!

But as **hard** as they tried,
things **did not** improve.
Would nothing bring back their
sparkling groove?

When the day of the Christmas show came around,
the fairies had done all they could.
But without their canes, they feared it was bound
to be boring and not any good!

Outside, the audience stood in line,
they just couldn't wait to get in.
The sisters hugged and said, "It's time.
Let's take a deep breath and begin."

Alone on the stage, the fairies sang,
softly at first, then stronger.
Slowly, they saw the joy they could bring –
they didn't need canes any longer!

There were no fancy sparkles,
music or lights,
just the fairies singing their parts.
But there was something special
that winter's night –
a magic that came from
their hearts.

As they finished their show, the audience **cheered**.
It had been a **wonderful** night.
The fairies bowed, then stepped outside
and were met by a **magical sight**.

Candy-cane stripes hung shining bright,
like ribbons from every tree.
They filled the sky with twinkling lights
as far as the eye could see!

Katie could barely believe it! Then, from behind a Christmas tree,

Judy the Garland Fairy cried out,

"I'm sorry, it's because of me!

I wanted the trees
to be beautiful
and sparkling
like your show.
So I took your stripes
without asking.
I've caused such trouble,
I know."

"What you did **was** wrong," said Katie,
"but you tried to do a **good** thing.

And tonight we've learned
we don't need our canes –
true sparkle
comes from within!"

Judy joined her friends in one last song
as it started to gently snow.

The fairies gathered and sang along –
this was the best-ever
Christmas show!

SHOW TONIGHT

Katie's Christmas show was saved by courage, love, and caring.

And that night, every fairy felt the joy that comes from sharing!

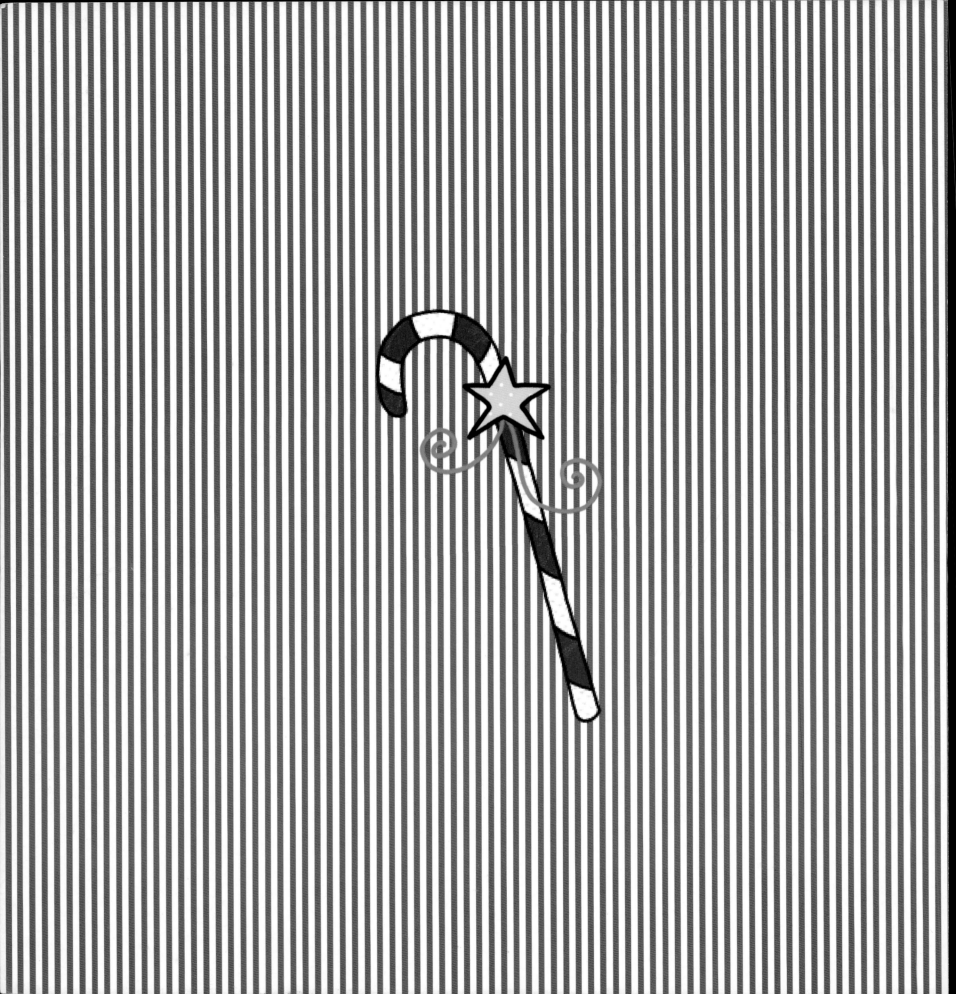